Peter Cohen · Olof Landström

Boris's Glasses

Translated by Joan Sandin

R&S
BOOKS

Stockholm New York London Adelaide Toronto

Rabén & Sjögren Bokförlag, Stockholm
www.raben.se

Translation copyright © 2003 by Joan Sandin
Originally published in Sweden by Rabén & Sjögren
under the title *Boris glasögon*
Text copyright © 2002 by Peter Cohen
Pictures copyright © 2002 by Olof Landström
Library of Congress Control Number: 2002096195
Printed in Denmark
First American edition, 2003
ISBN 91-29-65942-6

One night when Boris is sitting watching TV, he thinks the picture looks fuzzier than usual.

He calls a TV repairman.

"Nothing's wrong with your TV," says the repairman.
"The picture's fine. You've probably just gotten nearsighted.
Better go see an eye doctor."

The eye doctor examines Boris's eyes.
"Am I nearsighted?" asks Boris.
"Oh no," says the doctor.
"Then I'm farsighted?" says Boris.
"No, not at all! You have something else wrong with your eyes," says the eye doctor. "You're an astigmatic."
"Well, that's something!" says Boris. "Can you say that again . . . that thing that I am?"

"AS-TIG-MAT-IC," says the eye doctor.

"Aha," says Boris.

"It's probably hereditary," says the eye doctor. "You're going to need glasses. Please come back tomorrow."

An "astigmatic," well how about that! Boris says to himself as he walks to the bakery to pick up his turnip sandwiches.

An astigmatic, he thinks. It doesn't sound like something wrong. It sounds like something really fine . . . like someone who does something, like a certain kind of job.

There are bakers, shoemakers, and mechanics, thinks Boris.
And then there are astigmatics. And it's hereditary.

The next day Boris goes to get his glasses.

"Good heavens, how well I can see!" says Boris when he comes out on the street. "I had no idea there was so much to look at!"

He looks at the statue in the square and sees every single hair on the mayor's back.

He looks at babies in baby carriages and can even count their tiny fingers.

And he looks in the bakery window and can make out every little sugar rosette on the cakes.

"Oh, mercy me!" says Boris when he sees Gudrun in the bakery. "I had no idea Gudrun was so pretty!"

He feels so bashful that he forgets to pick up his turnip sandwiches.

Now that he sees so well, Boris decides he should get a job.
He goes to the big radio factory and asks if they need any help.

The manager becomes very interested when Boris tells
him he is an astigmatic.
"Have you been one for a long time?" he asks respectfully.
"Well, I should say so!" says Boris. "It's hereditary."
"We're always looking for clever people," says the manager.
"You can start in the plug department."

That must be the most important department in the whole
factory, thinks Boris, because if you can't plug the radio in,
no music will come out.

Boris gets to sit in a control booth with a big window and make sure that all the mice are working properly.
"It's just amazing how well I can see," says Boris, adjusting his glasses.

He looks to see if the plugs are put on right.
He looks to see if the cords are long enough.

He looks to see if the mice are testing the radios
correctly, and if the radios are actually playing
music when they're plugged in.

Boris gets a stiff neck from all the looking.

On the way home Boris works up the courage to pick up his turnip sandwiches.
"Well, if it isn't Boris!" says Gudrun. "I didn't know you wore glasses!"
"Well, yes, actually I do," says Boris. "I'm an astigmatic. It's hereditary."
"You don't say!"
Gudrun is totally impressed.

"Oh my," says Boris when he gets home. Everywhere he looks there are spider webs and dust bunnies and half-eaten turnip sandwiches.

I wonder if the programs weren't better before, Boris thinks.

On the second day Boris's eyes get really tired from all the staring. Sometimes he even thinks the mice are staring back at him. And the air in the control booth is bad, too.

In the afternoon he gets a terrible headache.
Well, I just can't sit here staring forever, Boris tells himself.

He takes off his glasses, fumbles for the door handle, goes out
of the control booth, past all the mice and all the radios . . .

. . . and out the factory gate.

"Good heavens, how lovely!" says Boris, looking around.
Everything is nice and fuzzy, just like he's used to.

At first Boris thinks of throwing away his glasses. But then he starts wondering if maybe it wouldn't be a good idea to keep them – for when he wants to count the fingers on little babies, or look at statues, or see the rosettes on cakes in the bakery. . .

". . . And for when I'm picking up my turnip sandwiches!"